Dear Parent:
Your child's love of reading starts here!

Every child learns to read in a different way and at his or her own speed. Some go back and forth between reading levels and read favorite books again and again. Others read through each level in order. You can help your young reader improve and become more confident by encouraging his or her own interests and abilities. From books your child reads with you to the first books he or she reads alone, there are I Can Read Books for every stage of reading:

SHARED READING
Basic language, word repetition, and whimsical illustrations, ideal for sharing with your emergent reader

BEGINNING READING
Short sentences, familiar words, and simple concepts for children eager to read on their own

READING WITH HELP
Engaging stories, longer sentences, and language play for developing readers

READING ALONE
Complex plots, challenging vocabulary, and high-interest topics for the independent reader

ADVANCED READING
Short paragraphs, chapters, and exciting themes for the perfect bridge to chapter books

I Can Read Books have introduced children to the joy of reading since 1957. Featuring award-winning authors and illustrators and a fabulous cast of beloved characters, I Can Read Books set the standard for beginning readers.

A lifetime of discovery begins with the magical words "I Can Read!"

*Visit www.icanread.com for information
on enriching your child's reading experience.*

I Can Read!

BEGINNING READING 1

Pinkalicious

Puptastic!

WITHDRAWN

For Woof

The author gratefully acknowledges
the artistic and editorial contributions
of Daniel Griffo and Justine Fontes.

I Can Read Book® is a trademark of HarperCollins Publishers.

Pinkalicious: Puptastic!
Copyright © 2013 by Victoria Kann

PINKALICIOUS and all related logos and characters are trademarks of Victoria Kann. Used with permission.

Based on the HarperCollins book *Pinkalicious* written by
Victoria Kann and Elizabeth Kann, illustrated by Victoria Kann
All rights reserved. Printed in the United States of America.
No part of this book may be used or reproduced in any manner whatsoever without
written permission except in the case of brief quotations embodied in critical articles and reviews.
For information address HarperCollins Children's Books, a division of HarperCollins Publishers,
10 East 53rd Street, New York, NY 10022.
www.icanread.com

Library of Congress catalog card number: 2012948580
ISBN 978-0-06-218786-4 (trade bdg.)—ISBN 978-0-06-218785-7 (pbk.)

13 14 15 16 LP/WOR 10 9 8 7 6 5 4 3
❖
First Edition

I Can Read!

BEGINNING 1 READING

Pinkalicious

Puptastic!

by Victoria Kann

HARPER

An Imprint of HarperCollinsPublishers

"I have news!" Mommy said.

"We are going to take care of a puppy.

The Razzles asked us to puppy-sit

Pinky this week when they are away."

Pinky and I will take long walks, chase butterflies, and play fetch.

PINK PUPPY PARK

8

"Taking care of Pinky will be pinkabulous!" I said happily.

"Pinky isn't really pink,"
said Daddy.

"She just has a pink nose."

"There's no such thing
as a pink dog," said Peter.

The next day, when the bell rang

I rushed to open the door.

"Hello, Pinky.

It's nice to meet you.

I am Pinkalicious!" I said.

11

Pinky didn't bark.

She didn't lick my hand.

When I tried to pet her, she hid!

12

"Pinky needs time to get used
to you," said Mrs. Razzle.
"I hope Pinky gets used to me soon.
I want to play with her!" I said.

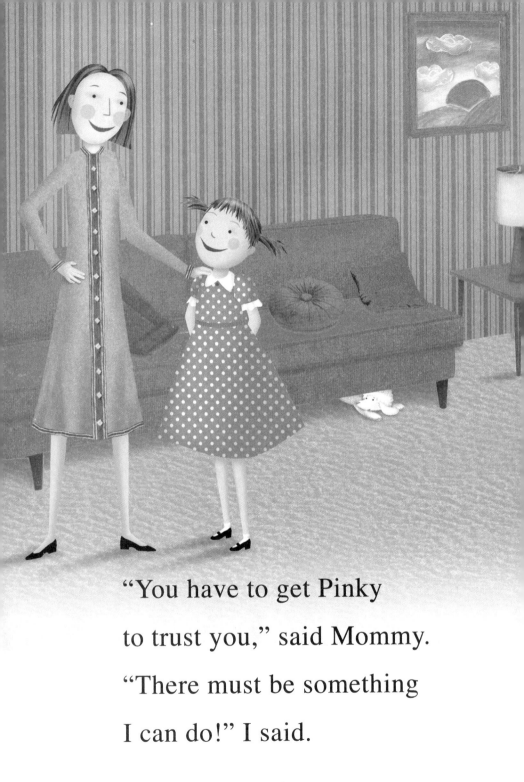

"You have to get Pinky
to trust you," said Mommy.
"There must be something
I can do!" I said.

14

I tried to make friends.

Pinky just hid under the sofa.

She did not come out!

Pinky didn't come out for a ball.
She didn't come out to see her bed.
She didn't even come out
for a dog treat I made her!
"Try taking Pinky outside,"
said Mommy.

I picked up Pinky and carried her

to the backyard.

Everything scared her,

even butterflies.

Worst of all, Pinky was scared

of me!

17

We went back inside,
but I didn't give up.
I tried to see things from
Pinky's point of view.

18

Everything looks bigger
when you crawl
on the floor!

Poor Pinky had the blues!

The next day I got an idea.

"I know what I like to do

when I feel blue," I told Pinky.

20

Pinky watched me fill the tub.

Her tail wagged.

"You must like bubbles, too!" I said.

Pinky jumped into the tub!

She snapped at the bubbles.

Oops!

Mommy's bottle of Pink

spilled into the tub.

The water turned bright pink.

22

Pink bubbles splashed all over!

Pinky snapped at the bubbles.

Pinky was very happy!

23

When Pinky got out of the tub

she was pink!

Pinky looked at her paws.

Then she turned around fast

to see her tail.

24

I told my family what happened.

"Now there really is such a thing

as a pink dog!" I said.

Pinky licked Peter in the face.

"Ewww!" said Peter.

27

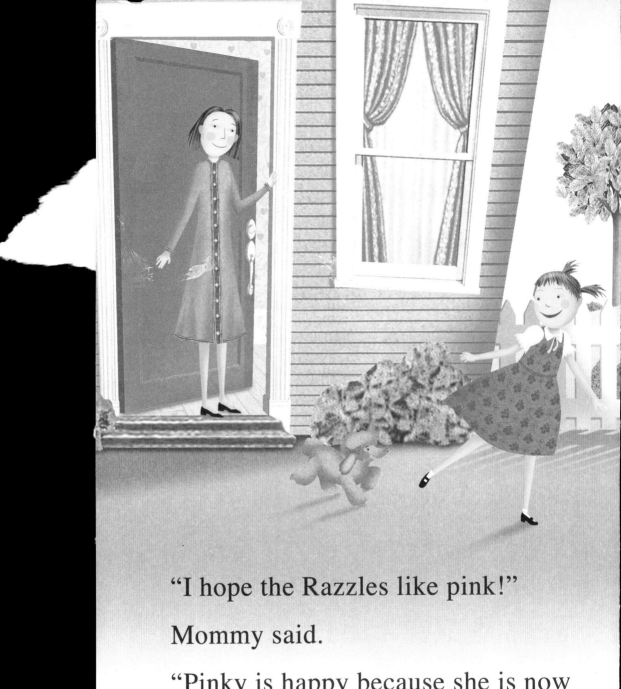

"I hope the Razzles like pink!"

Mommy said.

"Pinky is happy because she is now

as beautiful as her name!" I said.

28

The rest of the week went quickly.

Pinky and I took long walks

and played fetch.

We chased butterflies, too.

The Razzles were surprised to see

their puptastic dog.

Pinky is a pinkoodle now!

"I wonder if Pinky will stay pink,"

said Mr. Razzle.

I gave him a bar of green soap.

"Wash Pinky with this.

She will turn back to normal," I said.

I also gave the Razzles the ribbons.

"Pinky likes pink," I said.

"Maybe Pinky just likes you!"

said Mrs. Razzle.

Someday I hope I have a dog like Pinky.

For now, I'm just glad I helped make her happy.

32

31901059760613